RUDOLPH
THE RED-NOSED REINDEER®

By Alan Benjamin

Cover illustration by Paul Conrad • Interior pencils by Peter Emslie
Interior paints by Maria Claudia Di Genova and Valeria Turati

A GOLDEN BOOK • NEW YORK

© 2008 The Rudolph Company, L.P. Under license to Character Arts, LLC. All rights reserved. Published in the
United States by Golden Books, an imprint of Random House Children's Books, a division of Random House, Inc.,
1745 Broadway, New York, NY 10019, and in Canada by Random House of Canada Limited, Toronto.
Golden Books, A Golden Book, and the G colophon are registered trademarks of Random House, Inc.
Rudolph the Red-Nosed Reindeer © & ® The Rudolph Co., L.P.

www.goldenbooks.com   www.randomhouse.com/kids

Library of Congress Control Number: 2007939384   ISBN: 978-0-375-87511-3

PRINTED IN SINGAPORE
10 9 8 7 6 5 4

Hello, boys and girls. My name is Sam the Snowman. I'm going to tell you how Christmas was almost canceled one year, and how a little reindeer with a shiny red nose saved the day.

It all began in Christmastown at the North Pole. That's where Santa Claus lives with his wife, Mrs. Claus. Their home is a castle in the middle of a snow-covered forest of glittering Christmas trees.

Every Christmas, Santa delivers toys to good little girls and boys. And every Christmas, little reindeer dream of becoming part of Santa's team when they grow up.

Donner, one of Santa's reindeer, hoped his newborn son, Rudolph, would follow in his hoofsteps. But when Rudolph's nose began to glow, Donner cried, "He has a shiny nose! I'd even say it glows."

Just then, Santa arrived to meet the new reindeer. When he saw Rudolph's bright red nose glowing, he said, "Let's hope it stops, if he wants to make the sleigh team someday." And off he went.

"We'll just have to hide Rudolph's shiny nose so that he looks like all the other little deer," said Donner as he covered Rudolph's nose with mud. Rudolph was very unhappy, but he kept his nose hidden as well as he could.

Later, at the reindeer games, Rudolph met a pretty doe named Clarice. She was there to watch the young reindeer practice their flying. Rudolph was shy, but he asked if he could walk her home after the games. Clarice agreed and said, "I think you're cute." That made Rudolph so happy that he flew high in the sky on his very first try. Santa and Comet, the flying coach, were amazed!

But suddenly, Rudolph's false nose fell off and his real nose glowed brightly. All the other reindeer laughed and called him names, like Fire Snout and Red Schnoz and Rudolph the Red-Nosed Reindeer.

"From now on," said Comet, "we won't let Rudolph join in any reindeer games."

Rudolph was very sad, and he wondered why being a little bit different made him such a misfit. So he decided to run away.

Meanwhile, in Santa's castle, a team of elves made toys in a workshop. But one of the elves didn't like making toys—a blond elf named Hermey.

"Whatever is wrong with you, Hermey?" asked the Boss Elf.

"I don't like making toys," answered Hermey. "I want to be a dentist."

"A dentist?" barked the Boss Elf. "That's ridiculous. Elves make toys!"

Hermey was not about to give up his dream of becoming a dentist. So he decided to run away, too.

DENTISTRY

Soon the two misfits met and became good friends.

"Since we're both tired of being laughed at and called names, let's leave the North Pole and find out what the rest of the world is like," said Rudolph.

So off they went, looking forward to new adventures but knowing they had to beware of the Abominable Snow Monster of the North. The monster was mean and nasty and hated everything about Christmas.

"Cover your nose!" Hermey said to Rudolph when they heard the Abominable Snow Monster's horrible roar.

Before long, they ran into a prospector named Yukon Cornelius.
"This land is rich in silver and gold," he said. Yukon was an unusual
character, but he had a good heart and offered to give Rudolph and
Hermey a ride on his sled.

Suddenly, the Abominable Snow
Monster spotted the friends and
started to chase them.

"We're trapped!" cried Rudolph.
"My nose is giving us away!"

Luckily, Yukon knew the terrible
creature's weakness. "The Abominable
Snow Monster sinks in water,"
Yukon said as he quickly
chipped away at the ice.

    The three friends escaped on a sheet of floating ice and soon found themselves on the Island of Misfit Toys.

    King Moonracer, the flying lion who ruled the island, explained that every year he flew around the world to rescue misfit toys that nobody wanted. Each toy was free to live on the Island of Misfit Toys until some child decided to adopt it—because no toy could be truly happy until a boy or girl loved it.

Rudolph, Hermey, and Yukon met a Charlie-In-The-Box, a train whose caboose had square wheels, a polka-dot elephant, a cowboy who rode an ostrich, and a squirt gun that shot jelly. And there were many other misfit toys.

"Please ask Santa to include these wonderful toys with all the others he delivers on Christmas Eve," the king said to Rudolph.

"I promise I will," answered Rudolph.

That night, while his friends were sleeping, Rudolph decided to go on alone. He knew that the Abominable Snow Monster might find them all because of his bright red nose, and he didn't want to put his friends in danger.

During his journey, Rudolph began to realize he couldn't run away from his troubles. So he decided to go home.

In Christmastown, Rudolph discovered that his parents and Clarice had left to look for him and never returned. The little reindeer knew just where to find them—in the Abominable Snow Monster's cave!

"Put her down!" cried Rudolph as he tried to rescue Clarice. But then he was captured, too!

In the nick of time, Yukon and Hermey arrived with a plan. They knew that Abominable Snow Monsters love pork dinners, so while Hermey pretended to be a pig and oinked loudly, Yukon climbed above the entrance to the cave. When the monster came out, Yukon dropped a big chunk of ice on his head! That knocked out the Abominable Snow Monster, and Hermey finished the job by pulling out all of the creature's terrible teeth.

Rudolph and his friends returned to Christmastown. Everyone realized
they had been a little hard on the two misfits and welcomed them back.
At first, everyone was afraid of the Abominable Snow Monster. But
Yukon assured them that he was now as tame as a kitten, and that his
real name was Bumble. Everyone was relieved, and gave Bumble the
job of placing the stars on top of all the tall Christmas trees.

Rudolph described his adventures and told Santa about the Island of Misfit Toys. Santa promised he would deliver all the misfit toys to deserving girls and boys.

But there was terrible news—a great blizzard was raging
all over the world!

"I'm afraid," said Santa to Mrs. Claus, "that we'll just have to
cancel Christmas this year."

"Oh, no," said Mrs. Claus, "think of all those disappointed
little girls and boys with no presents on Christmas morning."

On Christmas Eve, the weather was no better, and there was no relief in sight.

Suddenly, Rudolph's nose started to glow. Santa shielded his eyes and smiled.

"That nose of yours," Santa said to Rudolph. "That beautiful, wonderful nose!"

"Rudolph, with your nose so bright, won't you guide my sleigh tonight?" asked Santa.

"I'd be proud to, Santa," answered Rudolph. Everyone cheered.

Even though the blizzard continued to howl, the elves got Santa's sleigh ready for takeoff. Santa put on his red suit, Rudolph and the other reindeer were harnessed with care, and Santa's sleigh was filled to the very top with toys.

"First stop is the Island of Misfit Toys," Santa said. "Ready, Rudolph?" "Ready, Santa!" Rudolph said, and his nose glowed as bright as a beacon in the night.

"Up, up, and away!" called Santa.
Off they flew into the dark sky to deliver toys to girls and boys—
with Rudolph's shining nose guiding the way.

And Rudolph went down in history as the most famous reindeer of all!